P9-CFW-989
3 5674 04593513 8

Letters to My Mother

GROUNDWOOD BOOKS
HOUSE OF ANANSI PRESS
TORONTO BERKELEY

Letters to My Mother

Teresa Cárdenas

Translated by David Unger

First published in Cuba as *Cartas al cielo*
First published in Canada and the USA in 2006

Groundwood Books / House of Anansi Press
110 Spadina Avenue, Suite 801, Toronto, Ontario M5V 2K4

Distributed in the USA by Publishers Group West
1700 Fourth Street, Berkeley, CA 94710

We acknowledge for their financial support of our publishing program the Canada Council for the Arts, the Government of Canada through the Book Publishing Industry Development Program (BPIDP) and the Ontario Arts Council.

Library and Archives Canada Cataloguing in Publication
Cárdenas, Teresa
Letters to my mother / by Teresa Cárdenas; translated by David Unger.
Translation of: Cartas al cielo.
ISBN-13: 978-0-88899-720-3 (bound) –
ISBN-10: 0-88899-720-5 (bound)
ISBN-13: 978-0-88899-721-0 (pbk.) –
ISBN-10: 0-88899-721-3 (pbk.)
1. Racism–Cuba–Juvenile fiction. 2. Cuba–Juvenile fiction.
I. Unger, David II. Title.
PZ7C196Le 2006 j863'.64 C2005-907011-0

Cover photograph by Manuel Cruzado Cazador
Design by Michael Solomon
Printed and bound in Canada

To Menú, Susy, Felipe and Mamá

I'd be better off up there with you.

Each and every night I wait for you to fly down on your paper kite and invite me to die once and for all.

It's March now. Flowers almost burst open at your feet when you look at them.

But you're not here.

I don't know how it happened, but my sketchbook is now full of words, shapes, phrases, memories and drawings—the drawings of a little girl putting her hand in her mother's, of a mother and father kissing each other, of the stars in Mamá's eyes, of Mamá playing among the clouds.

Dream pictures in my sketchbook.

They're all about you. You are in all of them.

Mamá, I don't know why you left me all alone,

without your kisses, your embraces, without the daisy scent that always trailed behind you…

I haven't told anyone how much I miss you. I can't bear much more of this silence. I'm going to begin writing to you…

Querida Mamá,

I saw you last night in my dreams. A lovely red ribbon was braided into your ponytail. You were running from one end of the sky to the other pulling a kite made of clouds.

You weren't happy, but there you were, running and skipping like a nine-year-old. You looked a lot like me, as if you were my daughter, not the other way around.

I called you many times in vain. It was sad.

I woke up in tears. No one came to ask me what was wrong.

I don't know why Tía Catalina bothers with me. She only cares about her daughters.

Lilita and Baby make fun of me all day long.

I wouldn't make fun of them if their mother died.

Mamita,

They're sending me to school here and I don't like it one bit. It's such a gloomy place.

I'm the tallest girl in the class, and the skinniest. Probably the saddest, too.

One of my classmates is named Sara. I don't know why her skin is light. Her father isn't like that.

Do you remember Pedro the carpenter? Well, Sara's father looks a lot like him. I think this embarrasses her because when he comes to school to pick her up or talk to the teacher, Sara pretends she doesn't know him. She walks off so that the rest of us won't think they are together.

A daughter shouldn't be embarrassed because her father is like Pedro the carpenter. Love has nothing to do with skin color.

Several classmates have accused Sara of

wanting to pass for a white girl. They say she's a *piola* who only likes white kids. That's because she likes Roberto, one of the white kids in class.

I think Sara is the most miserable one of us all.

Mamá,

Grandma says it's good to improve our race and the way to do that is to marry a white person. She herself wants to work for a white family as a maid. Tía Catalina says that's a dumb idea, but Grandma says that's all she's good for.

I don't think that's going to improve anything.

Querida Mamá,

There's something wrong with Lilita. Tía Catalina spends hours crying, and we've got to whisper when we're inside the house.

Lilita felt so bad one day that she didn't want to get out of bed. She couldn't recognize any of us.

Grandma said that someone had put a curse on her and that all of us had to be purified.

"Is Lilita going to die?" I asked worriedly.

She slapped me and said, "Shut up, *bembona*. You're a bad-luck bird." She pushed me away and followed Tía Catalina into the room where Lilita was tossing feverishly.

Since then everyone in this house where I don't want to be calls me *bembona* — thick lips!

Adorable Mamá,

Baby doesn't even talk to me anymore. Since she found out that we'd be going to school together, she pretends I'm not there. Before that, she and Lilita used to sing all the way to school and ignore me.

When we went out this morning, she didn't even give me her hand.

Baby is seven, and I'm three years older. I have to watch out for her, but she could care less.

She sticks out her tongue and says mean things. She does it just to make me angry. She knows that Tía Catalina would kill me if anything happened to her.

Mamita,

I found a piece of broken mirror on the street. All day long I stared at my forehead, my eyes, my nose and my mouth…

Guess what? I've discovered that my eyes are like yours — beautiful just as they are — and my mouth and nose are normal. I don't like it when people say that blacks are *bembones*, thick-lipped. If God exists, I'll bet he gets very angry when people criticize his creations.

What do you think I'd look like with blue eyes, a bony nose and a thin mouth? Ugly as can be — don't you agree?

That's why I won't let anyone run a hot comb through my hair. I don't want to look like Sara. I would even prefer to have cornrows, like African women.

When Lilita and Baby used to splash each other in the bathtub, they'd only splash below the waist so their hair wouldn't get wet and turn stiff.

Baby often goes around in a nightgown with a towel wrapped around her hair, shaking her head back and forth. "I have straight hair! I have straight hair!" she chants.

I laugh loudly, though it upsets me.

Some people don't know how to be black. How sad!

Lovely Mamá,

I've taken so many purifying baths. Grandma and Tía Catalina believe I've brought them bad luck.

They've put some strange-smelling herbs in my room. I also have to bathe in them, and put sweetwood bark and perfume in the water. The scent is okay, but the bark sticks to my skin and turns it the color of ash.

One day I rubbed sweetwood all over my face and messed up my hair.

Looking just like a ghost, I hid behind a door, waiting for Grandma to pass.

Then I jumped out and screamed, "Oooooooooooohhhhhh."

I scared her so much she nearly peed in her pants, but once she recovered, she just about killed me.

Mamita,

No one knows what's wrong with Lilita.

Grandma is half-crazy over it. She went all around the house shaking branches of herbs. Then she took a curse-remover branch, stirred it in whiskey and tobacco smoke and swatted us with it to purify us.

I was the last to get the treatment. She swatted me so hard that I still have bruises.

Dearest Mamita,

There's something very wrong with Lilita's spine.

Grandma bathes and feeds her, and at night tells her stories without letting her get out of bed.

Grandma's tired of coming up with cures. Darn! None of them seem to work. Once she brought over a lady wearing lots of necklaces. She looked like a rainbow.

I hid away to watch them. The lady took some things out of her shopping sack and spread them on the floor while Grandma took Lilita's clothes off.

They almost caught me when a dark baby chick jumped out of the sack and the lady chased it all around the room. I just about burst out laughing. Luckily the chick had a string tied to its foot. Otherwise it would still be running loose.

They smoked cigarettes and said some really weird prayers. Then the lady fell shaking to the floor, frothing at the mouth. She shrank up like a spool of thread.

Grandma kept asking her if she needed anything else to cure her grandchild. The lady answered hoarsely, "Babalú says that the *moquenquen* is cursed."

Grandma looked at Tía Catalina. "Didn't I tell you!"

The lady dragged herself to Lilita's bed and shook the chick and two burnt corncobs over her. "I've got to purify her first. I'll take care of the rest later."

Just then I sneezed loudly and everyone found out where I was.

They dragged me out by the ears.

Pretty Mamita,

Tía Catalina never talks about her daughter's father. Grandma says he's a no-good nothing. His name's Miguel and he's very bad tempered. He left one day and never came back.

"The farther away the better," Grandma said.

Tía Catalina continued scrubbing the floor. A bit later, Grandma cursed because she had lost track of time and hurried off.

She works for that white family I mentioned. She cooks, washes, irons and does whatever needs to be done. She's working herself to death, but she doesn't complain. On the contrary, she sings their praises though they pay her next to nothing.

Springtime Mamá,

They initiated Lilita to Babalú Aye to make her healthy again. Tía Catalina used up all her savings and borrowed what she didn't have. Grandma says that things aren't like before. "Everything was cheaper and easier before. A goat only cost two pesos!" She repeats the same thing over and over.

They initiated Lilita at the house of the lady who purified her. Lots of people showed up. I didn't see a thing because it was all a big secret. I spent all my time setting up the altar and helping in the kitchen, until Tía Catalina sent me to Menú's house to buy flowers.

Menú lives in a tiny wooden shack surrounded by a garden filled with plants and flowers. Menú is half crazy. She says she sells flowers because there are too many of them and they grow like weeds. She complains that their weird songs don't let her sleep at night.

Once a geranium grew so big in her bed she couldn't even lie down.

Can you believe it? She must think I'm a real fool!

There are lots and lots of flowers in her garden. I picked the prettiest.

White lilies for Obatalá, butterfly jasmines and sunflowers for Yemayá and Ochún, night-blooming jasmines for Oyá.

When I returned with the flowers, they had already begun slaughtering animals. You could feel the heat of their blood throughout the house.

One lady was afraid to snap her chicken's neck so she strangled it with a string.

Everyone ignored the chicken hanging in the middle of the garden, croaking softly.

We can't get the front door open because of all the offerings to Eleguá.

Whistles, caramels, marbles, cigarettes, small gourds filled with liquor, little dolls, coins — all kinds of things. Eleguá is a boy who's sometimes evil and sometimes good. That's why you have to give him things he likes, so he'll be good.

Every once in a while I slip a warm caramel in my mouth when no one's looking. Well, they'll rot soon enough. He can't eat them all!

Lilita looks better in her new dress. It's lavender, which is Babalú's favorite color. Grandma says he's merciful and cures the sick who believe in him.

Maybe he'll get Lilita to walk again.

Mamá,

Grandma's angry at me. She wants me to wash the clothes where she works. She says that I'll learn how to do something useful and the money I earn will help all of us out. I've spoken to her boss already. I don't want to work there, be someone else's maid.

But Grandma goes on and on about it and won't let me be.

I'm glad Tía Catalina spoke to her. Now she doesn't bother me as much.

So now I've got to clean and cook at home to earn my keep. That's what Tía Catalina says. But if you ask me this is no different than working for the "bosses."

Yesterday I played dumb and went out without doing any cleaning.

But Lilita made a huge fuss — the dust keeps her from breathing — and she said that I haven't swept in weeks. She says I'm just a spoiled, dirty brat like my mother.

I smacked her hard. I don't care if she can't get out of her chair.

Grandma and Tía Catalina heard her screaming and came running.

Mamá,

My back really, really hurts. Grandma whipped me like a slave. Menú, the old lady with the flowers, called her a beast. She brings herbs to heal my scars. They sure do stink, but they help ease the pain.

I've been punished. I can only leave my little room to cook. Tía Catalina doesn't want me near Lilita, or Baby, or anybody. Locked up here in my room the days never seem to end.

I look for you in the ceiling tiles, but it's no use. You're never there.

Before you used to glow in my room as if you were the moon.

I'd like to be far, far away from here, with you, in heaven.

Mamita,

Grandma dreamt about you. You told her nasty things in the dream and threatened to take her away with you.

I heard all about it.

Mamita, forget the flowers, the scented water, the coffee, the little plate of candies she set aside for you in the garden.

Take her, Mamita! Take her to that other world!

Mamá,

If you only knew what happened. I had to pee, but by the time I reached the bathroom, my panties were full of blood.

I got very, very scared.

Tía Catalina said that this happens to all women. According to her, I am a young lady now.

Grandma said that from now on, they'll have to keep their eyes glued to me so I don't end up pregnant.

What does that mean, Mamá? I don't think putting a piece of cotton between my legs will get me pregnant. That's not how it happens. First I've got to marry, buy a pretty house and be happy. Then the stork comes and inflates your belly. Everyone knows that.

So, nothing's changed. Same old, same old.

Mamita linda,

My head's about to burst. I've spent the whole day thinking about bellies and babies.

I remember when you told me that children make their parents happy. That's not my experience. You and Papá were happy till I was born, and then it all turned bad. I don't know what happened. You never told me.

You and I ended up living alone in a big old house. Then you ran out of money and we went to live in that awful, leaky house with so many people.

We stayed there till you went to heaven. I think you left because you were sick of the rain and the complaints, though I personally think that complaints are better than rain.

You'd spend the day saying that any moment

you'd go off and live where no one could find you. And that's exactly what you did.

Most people don't understand it, but I do.

Better to be in heaven than in an awful, leaky house.

You'd never be happy living there.

Mamá,

The old flower lady sent someone to get me this morning.

She's not feeling well. When I got there, she had a rag wrapped around her leg. "I'm lame," she told me. "I need your help." And since she's nice to me, I helped her. I cooked her a meal and picked leaves for her tea.

When I left her house, someone bumped into me. I almost fell down. I was about to give him a piece of my mind, but I was so surprised, I couldn't even open my mouth.

It was Roberto, the white kid in my class. He was in tears.

He started walking away from me when I picked up a few stray roses — I don't know why — and gave them to him.

At first he wouldn't take them. Then, in a whisper, he said thanks.

Ever since that day, he comes to Menú's house sometimes.

Most of the time he says nothing. He seems to have lots of problems.

Mamá,

People say that ghosts live in Menú's house. That's because her garden is like an enchanted forest.

There are shadows, flowers and birds all over the place.

At night, I can smell the garden scents in my room.

What a strange thing! It's as if I am being smothered by flowers.

She also has a huge ceiba tree.

Some people are afraid of her house. They say that a corpse is buried there. At first I thought it was a lie, but then she told me the whole story.

Menú lost her son when he was a baby. Somehow she buried him in the garden. Lots of flowers grow around the grave. She says that her son's body fertilizes the earth because he was planted, not buried. That's why the trees bear fruit year round. Even though she cuts back the plants with an old spade, they grow back overnight.

His grave is covered with pennies, marbles, roller skates and lots of other things. Lots of people come to ask him for favors and pray to him to make their sick children better. They even come all the way from Oriente Province. They say he works miracles.

Some people claim they have seen his ghost in the house or garden, flipping coins. At first Menú was angry and she'd throw rocks at whoever came by. But she grew tired of this and stopped.

Now she makes coffee for people who come from far away. I help her as much as I can. She's such an old lady. She seems more than a hundred years old.

Mamita,

I know why Roberto's sad. His mother goes out with lots of men just for the money. Sometimes she goes out and doesn't come back till the following day.

He doesn't want our classmates to hear about this. He made me swear not to tell anyone.

He told me that once she didn't come back for several days. When she did come back, she had bags under her eyes and was very thin. She spent the whole day crying and didn't go out for weeks.

Roberto says he would prefer not to have a mother than to have one running around like that. I'm not sure, but I don't think he really means it.

If I had you back, Mamita, I would never be ashamed of you.

Mamá,

The other day Grandma said she remembered her mother.

It was strange to hear her say mamá. She could barely pronounce the word. I had never considered she might have a mother, father or grandmother. Or that as a child she liked doing this or that.

She's always been so mean, ready to wallop me.

Grandma seems to have been born old and bitter, with no feelings.

Sometimes I want to take off her kerchief and stroke her white hair, hands, even her heart, but I'm afraid. She doesn't want affection from anyone. "What for?" she says. "You can't eat affection." I know she's lying because whenever she brings Baby candy she says, “You love your grandma, don’t you? Don’t you love me?”

And since Baby wants to eat the candy, she says yes, that she loves her a lot. This makes me sad. It’s as if Grandma is buying a bit of love.

I don’t love her at all. She’s always hitting me in the head. She never brings me sweets.

Dear Mamá,

Tía Catalina finally has a boyfriend.

His name is Fernando, and he's very light-skinned and has hair that's nearly straight. Grandma says she's lucky. Everyone really likes him, but I could take him or leave him. When he talks to me, it's usually something like, "Girl, bring me that ashtray," or, "Get me my coffee."

He thinks he's the master of the house, but I don't care. At least he doesn't call me *bembona.*

Mamá,

Fernando sleeps with Tía Catalina in her bedroom. As far as I know, they aren't married. At night I can hear the bed shaking. Tía Catalina starts moaning as if someone is killing her. And then she bursts out laughing like a kid.

The table has to be set when Fernando comes late in the afternoon. Grandma and Tía Catalina carry Lilita out and sit her next to him. She loves to hear his jokes and family stories. "It's better here," he says. "The people aren't as backward..."

Tía Catalina turns to molasses whenever he brings up marriage.

"I came to this town to start off right. I came looking for a pretty woman to marry. And who knows? Maybe I've found her." Grandma says that Tía Catalina has finally found happiness.

Sunny Mamá,

"Mr." Fernando eats his breakfast like a king. At first, coffee was enough. Now he wants bread, eggs and potatoes, juice and sweet rolls. Sometimes when Tía Catalina goes out early, Fernando takes Lilita breakfast and they talk for hours. It seems they've become good friends.

If I get to school late, the teacher just scolds me. Her name's Silvia and she's always laughing.

I'd like to be like her. She's very kind. She explains things over and over again until everyone understands. According to her, I'm very intelligent and that's why I'm going to make something of my life.

Precious Mamá,

Menú taught me how to pray and to say thc words just right so that God will hear me. God is good and merciful and very considerate. He got Mary pregnant without touching her, simply by releasing a fine golden rain over her body.

Then Jesus was born to save people from sin.

Sin is something that God doesn't like and yet people sin because they like to. Do you understand this?

At first, the people in his village said he was crazy, that he said stupid things. Some people tried to kill him while others wanted to hear his words.

Jesus looks like a nice man in the pictures. He's very white, with blue eyes and blond hair. Maybe he was born in France or in some other country like that.

Mamá,

I went to the school library, but couldn't find any books to explain this so I went into the church facing the park. Someone gave me a book that mentioned Jesus and the country where he was born. Mamá! He was almost born in Africa! Amazing, isn't it? Do you think that God can speak African? I don't think so. The old flower lady explained to me that Olofi is the name of the black people's God, but he's the same as the white God. Each group gives him the name and color they want. God made different-colored people because he is like a child bored by things that are all alike.

I don't think many white people know this story. They wouldn't want to pray to an inky-

skinned, fat-lipped God no matter how merciful
he was. They wouldn't find him handsome.

Dear Mamá,

Tía Catalina and Fernando went to a dance. They came back very late. She was drunk. Fernando put her to bed and went into the kitchen to have coffee. I heard him open the door to Lilita's room.

This seemed strange to me. So I went to see if something had happened to Lilita.

I froze.

Fernando was sitting on Lilita's bed and looking at her like some fool. Her robe was open and she held her head down in shame.

I didn't sleep a wink the whole night. If I told Tía Catalina, she wouldn't believe me. She prefers ignorance to loneliness.

I'd better bite my tongue and be careful. Very careful, so he doesn't decide to come and visit me as well.

Mamá,

I ovcrslcpt and wc got to school latcr than cvcr.

The teacher scolded Baby. She glared at me as if she wanted to kill me.

After school, I looked for Baby all over. I looked for her in the garden, our hideouts, the bathrooms and the backyard.

Tía Catalina would kill me if I came home without her.

But I made such a fuss that they didn't punish me.

Tía Catalina was waiting for me by the door. Her face said it all. "You got off lucky because nothing happened to her," she said. "Otherwise, no one would have stopped me from beating you to death."

I sighed in relief.

When I entered the house, she pinched me hard. “Straighten up. If this happens again, you’ll end up living with Grandma!”

I didn’t leave my room that night. I didn’t want Tía Catalina to remember about sending me to Grandma’s house.

I thought they would scold Baby for leaving school without me, but they didn’t say a word to her. Grandma took her for a stroll, saying that all kids do what she had done.

I locked myself in my room and dreamt I was a queen and had servants that brought me bread pudding in bed.

Mamá,

Roberto sometimes shows up at Menú's house in the afternoon. When he isn't running errands, he brings her a barrel of water or he digs holes in the garden for her new plants.

He says he prefers to stay with us than to be at home and see his mother going out in tight dresses.

Menú likes him and always makes him a lemonade or a milkshake.

Sometimes we lie on the ground and look for cloud animals and other things in the sky. That's how we pass the time.

"I see…a man walking a dog," he says.

"I see a little boat on a wave," I answer.

"I see a giant palm tree."

"I see a flower basket, a guitar, a broken shoe,

a gourd full of pens, a woman saying goodbye, a polar bear."

And then, Mamá, I saw you running among the clouds as usual. Roberto said, "I see...a little girl holding a kite!"

I kissed and hugged him a lot. He looked at me as if I were crazy. I felt embarrassed, but I think he liked it.

Mamita,

Today is your birthday. You are thirty-seven years old. No one here says a thing, but I know they remember. Grandma showed me a photo of you that I had never seen before. You were a little girl, pursing your lips as if you were angry about something.

Grandma put some jasmines — your favorite flowers — under the photo.

Tía Catalina didn't let me work today. She made me breakfast and cleaned the house herself.

This must be the day of miracles.

Mamá,

Sara's leaving our school. Her father got a job in another province. We found out this morning when we saw them speaking to the director. Sara's head was hanging down.

Sara will never change.

There are people who will never change even when they want to.

Mamita,

A few weeks ago Fernando came home drunk and almost killed Tía Catalina.

He pushed her into the patio and hit her a lot. Luckily Grandma wasn't home or she'd have gone into a fainting fit.

Tía Catalina slept with Baby that night. The following day Fernando was nowhere to be seen. I don't think she breathed a word of this to Grandma, though I'm sure she suspects something happened.

Two weeks later Fernando showed up, dirty and unshaven. He looked twenty years older. Without saying a word to anyone, he went into the bedroom and stayed there the whole afternoon.

Tía Catalina ran water for his shower and

gave him something to eat as if he were a little boy. That night, the bed didn't stop shaking — *boom, ta boom, boom, ta boom, boom, ta boom.*

Mamá whom I miss,

Before we got to school, Baby stopped and looked me over as if I were a strange insect. "You sure are skinny and *bembona,*" she said to me.

And what did she do next? She spat on me.

I was about to punch her, but I remembered what had happened to Lilita and I stopped.

I simply walked away from her. I didn't want her to see me crying.

I went to Menú's house and stayed there all day.

After sundown, Grandma came to look for me with a stick.

Menú and Grandma started screaming at each other. It was awful to see two old women nearly coming to blows. And all because of me.

Grandma chased me around the yard with the stick. I hid behind Menú's son's grave. Grandma swung the stick at me, but broke off the wooden cross on top of the grave in one fell swoop. Menú began screaming and pulling Grandma's hair. I burst out laughing. Seeing me laugh, Grandma let go of Menú and threw the stick at me.

Everything turned black.

When I woke up, I was in the hospital and needed five stitches.

Menú said it would be better if I spent a few days with her.

At night I dream that the wind is blowing and carrying all my things to the sky.

My head hurts so much it's killing me. I can't think about anything.

Mamá,

Silvia has taken a liking to me. She asked Tía Catalina for permission for me to spend the weekend with her.

To reach her house, we have to cross the city. Silvia lives with her father who is very old and needs reading glasses.

As soon as I got to her house, he gave me a book. I don't think I'll ever read it because it's too thick. Silvia laughed and said no matter how smart I am, I wouldn't understand a thing in it.

The book is from France. Did you know that there is a big country called France? Silvia says that it's a very cultured place, quite advanced. Lovers kiss on the street and no one says a thing because it's absolutely normal.

Mamá, I want to go to France! I want to see the famous tower there. I've been told that you can see all of France from the top.

Mamá in the clouds,

Roberto doesn't believe that people go to heaven. He says they simply die and that's it. I've tried to explain it to him a few times, but he doesn't get it.

You can't see heaven, you can only feel it. You can't even imagine such a beautiful and peaceful place. And if you can, what you imagine is different from what someone else might. Each person has his own heaven.

I believe it's a place where no one lies and where everyone gets along.

I want a heaven where grandmothers are kind and give candy to their grandchildren. Where no one mistreats children or makes them do things they don't like. A heaven where no one calls me *bembona* or ugly and where I wouldn't feel so all alone.

For me, heaven is full of the things you want most. It doesn't matter if you want a person or not, if she's dead or alive.

I want the kind of heaven where Roberto, Menú and her son, Silvia, you and I can play games forever and ever.

Mamita,

For a while now, Grandma has been talking to herself and looking at Fernando out of the corner of her eye. He ignores her, hardly leaving his room. But when night comes, he dresses up and goes out. Tía Catalina says nothing, locks herself in the bedroom and we don't see hide nor hair of her until the following day.

Whenever I see Fernando, I remember what he did to Lilita. I want to tell Tía Catalina or Grandma...but I'm afraid to.

I've felt sorry for my cousin ever since then. But because I can't explain what happened, once in a while I take my cot to her room to keep her company.

At first she thought it was a bit strange, but said nothing. When Tía Catalina told me to get out, Lilita said that she didn't want me to leave.

Fernando found out one night when he came into the room when Lilita was sleeping and saw me sitting on my cot.

He acted all innocent and asked how Lilita was doing. I told him that she was fine and began to read a book. Then he left.

This afternoon Grandma came home very angry. She grabbed Tía Catalina by the arm and dragged her to the back of the house. I could hear them shouting back there. Grandma wants Tía Catalina to kick Fernando out. They argued back and forth for a long time.

Then Grandma slammed the door and left.

Dearest Mamita,

I was playing and jumping around at recess when one of the big boys started teasing me about my braids. I tried to ignore him, but he kept saying mean things no matter where I went in the playground.

Then he pulled on my braids.

Suddenly, Roberto came out of nowhere and pounced on him like a wildcat.

All our classmates started shouting.

The mean boy was really big, but Roberto didn't care. They punched each other a lot. Roberto was black and blue, with scratches all over his body. The other boy was also injured. This is the first time anyone has ever defended me.

If he asks, I'll be his girlfriend.

It's nice having someone stand up for you. It's great to feel that someone cares.

Mamá mia,

When Roberto and I go for walks, I don't want him holding my hand because people stare as if we are doing something weird. He got angry with me and said he doesn't care what others think. "People always talk," he said. And it's true. Each time Grandma talks about the family where she works she says the white folk this or the white folk that, or that white woman told me such and such. That's how she speaks about them.

"Who's that little white boy you're always with?" she asked once. I didn't know what to say. I even forgot that Roberto is white.

That's when I learned that when you love someone, skin color doesn't matter. And it's nicer to say "Roberto" than "that white boy."

Mamita,

Tía Catalina ignores us all — Grandma, her daughters, everyone.

She paces back and forth all day, vomiting whatever is in her stomach.

Everything makes her nauseous — eggs, garlic, lentils. I don't know what to cook since she throws it all up.

I told her she should see a doctor but she won't listen to me.

We take Lilita to the hospital twice a week. They shine a light on her back and make her do strange leg exercises. There are lots of people there who have trouble walking. I take her because we're getting along a bit better now.

In the afternoon I tell her what happened at school. One day she said she wanted to meet Menú.

When she lets me, I comb her hair in different styles using lots of colored clips. I don't feel sorry for her anymore.

She's grown to be a very pretty young lady. And she's so smart. She'll certainly get a job that will make her famous — maybe become a writer or a radio broadcaster.

She's a strong young lady, not afraid of anything.

Mamá,

Everyone says that Fernando left the country. Tía Catalina doesn't want to believe it and she's combed through the neighborhood two or three times. She even went to the house of another woman he was seeing by the harbor. But no one knows where he's hiding.

She looks for him in bars, at his best friends' houses, at his godfather's house. He's nowhere to be found. It's as if the ground swallowed him up. And since he's not in a hospital or a jail, she now believes what people say. Still she spends most of the day waiting by the door for news of him.

The vomiting goes on and she's growing fat. Her clothes don't fit her anymore. She only wears a huge dress that looks more like a robe.

Mamita,

I haven't seen Grandma for days. She's got heart problems.

Tía Catalina says she should visit her, but she's only gone there three times.

The doctor prescribed rest and quiet. She has to take care of herself.

It wasn't easy work finding Grandma's house. I don't know how she can live in such a small house. One long step and you cross the bedroom. One more step and you're in the kitchen.

"I'm just a worn-out horse," she said to me just before falling back asleep.

I made her a vegetable broth and waited for her to wake up.

As I watched her, she seemed to be someone

else, so still and quiet. I don't know why she's so mean to me. I never did anything to her.

I sometimes wonder what it would be like if we got along. If we actually loved one another.

Mamá, what would Grandma's kisses taste like?

Mamá in heaven,

Now I know who my father is.

Grandma blurted it out as if someone had been strangling her. She says she wants to leave this world with no secrets and no regrets.

She blurted it out and I still don't believe it.

How can I believe that "the bad-tempered no-good Manuel" is my father? How can I accept that Lilita and I have the same father? According to Grandma, you took Tía Catalina's peace of mind away from her. Since then she's had bad luck with men. "Not even with Baby's father, who was good at the beginning."

"They're all alike. The best of them should be killed," she said.

Grandma had no news from you for a long time. And when I was born, she took it out on me. According to her, each time she looks at me she remembers all of it. I don't know what you would have done if someone had done that to you. It's been hard for Tía Catalina.

But if Manuel fell in love with you, it was because he didn't love her anymore. That's why he took you far away from here.

The bad thing is that later he left you, too. He just took off. Disappeared.

You wanted to go to heaven because you couldn't put up with him anymore.

You left not thinking about me and how much I would miss you.

I want to be angry at you, but I can't. I love you so much. I'm always dreaming of you coming down from the sky in starched white clothes, with jasmines and red hibiscus flowers braided into your dark hair. "I want to come back," you say to me, but I wake up knowing you won't, even if I were to ask it of you a thousand times.

Mamita,

Roberto's helping me look for Papá.

I know it won't be easy. Neither Tía Carolina nor Grandma have any idea where he might be.

Grandma says that since he was a railroad worker, he could be living anywhere on the island right now. "God knows."

I'm scared of meeting him and finding out he wants nothing to do with me or that he's a good-for-nothing drunk.

No matter how many times I turn it over in my head, I don't understand why he left as he did, suddenly, saying nothing to anyone.

If Papá showed up, I don't know what would happen. When I close my eyes, I see a big, strong man walking around the house with lots of packages in his arms. I don't know why I see him like that.

I know his name is Manuel Ocanto, and that everyone calls him Cargo Train because he's strong, and that he lives somewhere in Cuba. Roberto says we're going to find him no matter what. "How many people do you know with the nickname Cargo Train?" he asks, laughing. And I believe we're going to find him, even if it's at the last train station in the world. And I'm doing this for Lilita as well as myself, since she's dying to put her arms around him.

We'll start looking for him at the train station here. Maybe someone knows where he lives.

Bright light Mamá,

Time flies and not because I am having fun. I'm fifteen years old now and have I grown. If you were to see me, you'd know how much I've changed. After so much braiding, my hair has grown out! It looks a lot like yours did. Each day I look more like you, Grandma says.

I'd like to be a teacher, but Lilita says I should cut hair, that my hands are magical.

All I know is that I love teaching children, seeing how they learn things they'll never forget, knowing they'll remember me, their teacher. Just as I remember Silvia — my good, kind Silvia.

Things have also changed at home.

Tía Catalina finally found a "good man," and she went off to live with him. She only took Fernandito with her.

She comes back to visit every once in a while and stays two or three days before going back.

Baby is huge! She decided to go to a special sports school. She hasn't changed all that much. She's stubborn, just like Grandma.

With Lilita, it's another story. It's amazing how hard she's been trying to find Papá. She's got so many ideas. She's already made a list of all the towns in Cuba with railroad stations. And she's written more than twenty letters to the station-masters asking them if they've heard of him.

We've learned to treat one another like sisters. We've forgiven one another for so many things.

Now she says that she will definitely be a writer. She sends her poems to all sorts of contests, but she has yet to win. She says she won't give up.

Once she read me some of her poems. They are really quite beautiful — and sad. Just recently she wrote a couple of short stories about the family.

She won't send those out. They're just for the family.

I've been thinking about giving Lilita a gift —

something that will make her really happy. I've begun saving up.

I want to buy her a typewriter — a very old typewriter — so at least she won't have to write by hand anymore.

As for Grandma, well… She's learned to live with both her sick heart and with me.

She hardly does anything at home now. There are times she's stubborn as a mule and we have to let her do what she wants.

She's lived with us since her last heart attack, which scared the life out of us. She almost died.

It isn't easy, but I'm beginning to understand her better. I even love her a little bit. Sometimes that old crone is like a difficult puzzle and there's no God who could understand her. Some days she's calm and others she's like a tornado whirling around the house.

Every once in a while she visits the corner of the courtyard where the dead are buried and she lights a candle. She won't admit it, but she prays for forgiveness and to forgive others.

When she's feeling good, she walks around the block or visits Menú. She says that because they are both crazy old women, they see eye to eye. I'd like to go with her, but she doesn't let me. She doesn't want pity from anyone.

I look at her and wonder if she remembers everything she did to me, all that I suffered because of her. I think she does because there's really no way to forget.

Roberto and I are still good friends. Well, not just friends, but boyfriend and girlfriend. When we don't go to the movies, we go to a spot by the sea or to Menú's "enchanted forest."

He's studying to be some kind of tree doctor. I never imagined that trees and flowers had such exotic names. He studies a lot, but always sets aside a bit of time to help us write letters to the stationmasters and to help his sweet old lady, Menú.

His mother married a Spaniard about a year ago and moved to Spain, though she writes that she misses Cuba a lot and that Spain is nothing like home.

Mamita,

Last night you were in my dreams again. You were saying goodbye to me.

As Menú says, the light finally reached your soul and your spirit is rising.

You were there, with your kite, smiling at me.

Then all of a sudden you began to grow and grow and were transformed into thousands of tiny birds that filled the sky.

Mamá, even though I wish you were here with me and not where you are, so far away, I want you to know that I forgive you.

I forgive you for all the days you weren't with me and for all the days to come. I know that you will take care of me from heaven.

Don't worry. I'm fine. Soon we will find Papá.

All the pain will be left behind.

We will see each other again, Mamá.
Goodbye.
I love you so much.

YOUR DAUGHTER

GLOSSARY

Babalú or *Babalú Aye*: God who corresponds to the Christian St. Lazarus and is one of the Orishas, or guardian spirits. Much adored in Cuba and prayed to for good health.

Bembona: Pejorative reference to black people with thick lips.

Eleguá: Yoruba god of both luck and misfortune.

Moquenquen: Small child in Yoruba, the language spoken by most of Cuba's slaves.

Obatalá: Orisha god of peace and wisdom.

Ochún or *Oshún*: Goddess of love, happiness and femininity.

Olofi: The Supreme God for Afro-Cuban believers.

Oyá: Goddess of cemeteries and spirits.

Piola: Pejorative, refers to people who prefer white people as friends.

Yemayá: Yoruba god, universal mother, ruler of the fish and the seas.